Some more thought-provoking
questions you'll find in

HOW TO GET
YOUR KIDS TO TALK:

- Do you think it's a good idea for people to date if they work together or go to school together?

- What is your greatest accomplishment so far?

- Mom, what went through your mind when you found out you were pregnant with me? What did you think when you first saw me?

- When do you have more fun—when you're with your friends of the same sex, or when you're with your girlfriend or boyfriend? Explain.

- If you were to change your mind about someone you were dating, and wanted to break up with that person, how would you go about it?

HOW TO GET YOUR KIDS TO TALK

The Question Game for Young Adults

Joyce L. Vedral, Ph.D.

BALLANTINE BOOKS • NEW YORK

Library of Congress Catalog Card Number: 93-90705

ISBN 0-345-37372-3

Manufactured in the United States of America

First Edition: February 1994

– DEDICATION –

To the young adults—the future leaders of our nation. May you continue to question and to think. May you learn to tolerate opinions that differ from your own. May you never cease to express your own unique view of things.

– TABLE OF CONTENTS –

– ACKNOWLEDGMENTS –

To the teenagers and young adults of America—ranging in age from thirteen to twenty-one—who contributed your questions to this book.

To Marthe Simone Vedral and Jennifer Berkowitz, for your special contributions to the question game.

To Bob Wyatt, former editor-in-chief of Ballantine Books, for your concern for the youth and for your continued support and encouragement.

To Jim Freed, former Ballantine editorial assistant, for your efficient handling of matters related to this book.

To Jennifer Richards, my former Ballantine East Coast publicist, to Liz Williams, head of West Coast publicity, and to Marie Coolman, her assistant, for going the extra mile. You could not possibly be overpaid for the job you are doing.

To Pam Bernstein, my editor at the William Morris Agency, for your buoyant spirit, your sense of humor, and for your handling of this project.

To family and friends, especially Randie Levine, Cameo Kneuer, Carol Acker, and Irma Drosh, for your continual support.

– TO THE PARENTS:
HOW TO USE THIS BOOK! –

When you open to chapter one, at first, you may be a bit confused. "I thought I was reading a book for parents—why does she seem to be addressing teens?" The answer is simple, and, in fact, *the very key to the book*. The book is addressed to teens, because after reading it yourself, and paying very special attention to the note to you on page 116, you're going to hand the book over to your teen and let your teen take it from there!

My strategy is simple. After dealing with teenagers for twenty-some-odd years, I discovered that if you're going to get a teen to do anything, that teen must be motivated to do it because he/she thinks, "I like this idea. This can really help me," and not because mom or dad decides so, and *especially* not because mom or dad says something like, "Let's communicate."

Before you can get your kids to talk to you—to play the game with you—it may be necessary to get them excited about the game and how it works with friends and with the opposite sex. Once they're "hooked on the game," and they see how much fun it is, chances are they will be nudging you to play it with them so that they can, in their own minds, "see where you're coming from."

There's another option. You may be able to engage your teen more directly. One day, while sitting around the living room with your teen, say, "I have a question-game book here—can we play it for a few minutes? Pick a number from one to fifty." Then ask the question from chapter six, questions for parents to ask teens. Once the teen answers, say, "Now I pick a number from one to fifty (handing him the book open to chapter five, questions for teens to ask parents). Then pick a number, have your teen read you the question, and you answer it.

The fun of the game is, neither you nor your teen will know what question will be asked (unless, of course, you have memorized the questions and their corresponding numbers). Remind your teen that, according to the rules, you both have to answer the question candidly—or the fun goes out of the game.

After you and your teen have had fun with the book, see if you can ignite a game between your teen and his/her grandparents the next time you have a family gathering. Later, if your teen has not already taken possession of the book, you can give it to him/her and let him/her play the game with peers and other adults. Before you know it, all kinds of communication will have begun—and in a very fun way.

1

The Question Game

We had gone over to Kim's house to watch
some horror videos. There were six of us altogether. While we were waiting for my friend
Joe to arrive, someone opened up the question
game book [an early draft of the book you're
holding] and read a question. Before you know
it, we were all talking a mile a minute. Three
hours later, Joe had arrived, but we were still
playing the game. It was past midnight and we
never did get to see the videos. Wow. What I
learned about people that night—I even saw a
different side to my boyfriend. Something to really think about.

Trish, 17

Warning: If you're afraid of "getting deep,"
don't play the question game—because even if you
try not to, after about ten minutes into the game,

you'll find yourself exchanging ideas, wishes, dreams, hopes, fears, angers, indignities, and indeed, philosophies. The time will fly. Like Trish, you'll look up and three hours will have passed. You'll wonder where the time went.

In this day and age people rarely delve below the surface, instead spending too much time watching others have revelatory experiences on a screen. The question game could be an oasis in this emotional desert. It provides a natural, mind-awakening atmosphere in which you can spout off opinions, dig deep into the ideas of others, and within hours get to know people at a level that might otherwise take you months, or even years, to reach. What's more, it produces the kind of excitement you feel only when you're exercising your mind and stretching your imagination beyond its usual limits. There is no exaggerating the excitement and thrill of probing deep into your own thoughts and the thoughts of others.

In short, if you play the question game with someone, you will tear down the walls between you. You'll need courage. The game isn't "safe." But it's informative, and it's fun.

- WHAT THE GAME WILL DO FOR YOU -

The question game is empowering. After playing it for a while, you begin to learn to "read" people (those with whom you play the game). You gain insight into their value systems, fears, angers, motivations, etc. Sometimes you are enabled to take an educated guess as to how people will behave toward you in the future.

In addition, you'll learn a lot about yourself. As you play the game, you too will be answering questions, and as you speak, you will "hear yourself talk." You will begin to listen to yourself, perhaps for the first time, and in the listening, you'll discover for yourself where you *really* stand on certain issues. (Don't be surprised to hear yourself think, "I didn't know I thought that!")

What's more, your answers to the questions posed will be displayed in front of you in comparison with and in contrast to the answers of others playing the game. This experience will prove priceless. You'll be testing and sharpening your ideas and opinions against those of others. In the end, your original opinions will be reinforced or modified or altogether changed. But no matter what, your range of thought will be expanded and your mind opened. You will find yourself less inclined to be rigidly opinionated.

To be opinionated is to hold unreasonably or obstinately to your own idea; to refuse not only to consider another point of view, but even to allow that another point of view can exist—to the point where you judge or condemn the person for even having a different opinion (specifically, one that is offensive to you).

Being opinionated can cause you to remain stagnant in your thinking. It's a posture that can keep you bound for the rest of your life to decisions you made about issues when you were ten years old—or to ideas you learned from parents, brothers, sisters, etc.

After playing the question game for a while, you may find that where you used to find yourself immediately saying "That's ridiculous" when someone expressed an idea diametrically opposed to yours, you now find yourself saying, "Hmm. I never thought of it that way." And instead of writing a person off as soon as he or she disagrees with you, you may find yourself wanting to retain that person as a friend—whether or not the two of you agree on every point.

The best part of it all is, you will spend less energy fighting unnecessary battles, making unnecessary foes. You will learn a precious lesson at an early age: to live and let live. In effect, you will save your energy for the real battles in life.

– GAIN INSIGHT INTO THE
ONE YOU ARE DATING –

Let's be more specific. If you use the question game either with a new interest, say a casual date, or with your long-term boyfriend or girlfriend, you'll learn a lot. You'll find out about the pain and suffering that person has endured in order to make him or her the person you see in front of you. You will find out what makes that person happy or sad. You will also discover why he or she is attracted to you, and what's more, you'll feel either pleased or disappointed at the discovery.

You'll gain deep insight into your boyfriend's or girlfriend's values (what things in life does that person prize, or find to be "right"). This information alone can draw the two of you closer together—or it can further distance you from one another. Once you start playing the game, you'll see exactly what I mean; but if you want to put your imagination to work immediately, pause here and skim the "dating" chapter (which begins on p. 28).

– SEE HOW OTHER TEENS OF BOTH SEXES FEEL ABOUT INTERESTING ISSUES—AND MAKE NEW FRIENDS ALONG THE WAY –

Sparks will fly when you play the question game in a group of mixed company—whether you're with guys and girls you've known for a long time or a bunch of people you've just met. Girls will find out what bothers guys about girls, and guys will find out what bothers girls about guys. Everyone will gain insight into the depth or shallowness of other people's thinking. In fact, some will come away thinking, "I never knew so-and-so was so spiritual, or deep, or intense." Others may say, "That person certainly wasn't brought up the way I was." All will welcome and enjoy, but more important, all will enjoy the chance to air their views on various topics. The energy that passes through the group during the game will provide the natural high we all enjoy experiencing.

– DEEPEN YOUR FRIENDSHIPS –

If you play the question game with your friends, you can find out how much loyalty and honesty you can expect in the future. You can also find out why any given two of you are friends in the first place. How so?

By finding out that, say, you and your friend share the same views on issues you've never discussed before. By learning what experiences your friend has had in early childhood and beyond, you will gain invaluable insight into your friend's personality. And of course, it's a two-way process: You will be able to reveal yourself to your friend in a way that usually doesn't offer itself in everyday conversation. The bond between the two of you will be strengthened.

– FIND OUT ALL ABOUT YOUR PARENTS—AND GET CLOSER TO THEM IN A NATURAL WAY –

What? Parents? No way!

Think again. Playing the question game with parents can be the best thing you've ever done for yourself—and for them. It can help you to understand, finally, what makes your parents feel a certain way about things, and why they say and do some things you now cannot understand. It will take at least some of the mystery out of why they seem overconcerned about things that strike you as relatively unimportant. It will help you to see that your parents too have goals, dreams, worries, and disappointments. In truth, it will cause you to look at your parents with more compassionate eyes.

You will learn a lot about how your parents felt when they were teens. You may even discover some of the mischievous or downright outrageous things your parents did as as teens—and how your grandparents reacted to such behavior. What's more, you'll find out how your parents felt, when they were growing up, about *their* parents.

On the other side of the coin, your parents will be given an opportunity to see and accept you for what you are—as *you* answer questions posed in the game. All of this will be done in such a natural, fun way that there will be no real embarrassment at either end of the generation gap (which will have narrowed). By the end of a game-playing session, your parents will be thinking, "I never really knew my own child. I'm amazed."

The simple fact is, playing the question game with your parents will help even the most perceptive and understanding parents to see new aspects of your personality and emotional makeup, ones perhaps completely different from theirs, and to begin to accept those differences. The game-playing will help them to come to terms with the fact that even though you are their child, you are a completely separate individual—an adult in the making. They may well reflect that just as they are different from their parents—and that this is a right and a good thing—so you are different from them, and that this too is right and good. This realization is bound to improve your relationship with your parents.

– ESTABLISH A CLOSER RELATIONSHIP WITH YOUR GRANDPARENTS, AND A DEEPER RESPECT FOR THEM –

For those of you who have even one grandparent alive (many of you have all four): How lucky you are! What a treasure it is to have a blood relative who has the advantage of having been alive when the history of our present world was still very much in the making.

You can find out many things from your grandparents. For instance, you can discover how it felt to live in a world without television, headphones, videotapes, computers, and in some cases, even the telephone.

But grandparents can give you more than an eyewitness account of history. They can impart to you the most valuable gift of all, that of wisdom. They've seen a lot of things in their time. They know more than you can imagine, and the question game will bring this knowledge out in a natural way.

If you play the question game with your grandparents, you'll find out from yet another angle how your parents felt as teenagers, and you may be surprised to learn that even they gave their parents a "hard time."

The question game will also help your grandparents to get to know you. Where they would otherwise hesitate to intrude on your life, the game makes talking about you and your interests a natural thing. Older people often feel distanced from the younger generation, and even shut out. The question game will help to bridge the gap. As you answer the questions, you'll find yourself talking about the world you live in, as your grandparents listen with rapt attention. You'll find that they are delighted to be "educated" by you, and are more than eager to learn what is going on today.

All of this communication will help to build a special bond between you and your grandparents, a bond that you will greatly appreciate now, and even more after they are gone. You simply can't put a price on that.

– HAVE SPONTANEOUS MIND FUN WITH ANYONE AT ANY TIME –

The next to last chapter in this book is a game you can use (in theory) with anyone. You can use it with other relatives, with teachers, parents or friends, bosses, co-workers, even strangers—

anyone who is willing to have some informative fun. (Of course you can always try it out on sweethearts, friends, parents, and grandparents, in addition to the question games designated specifically for them.)

Playing the game will open up a wide range of discussion and give you the opportunity to see how other people think on a variety of issues.

– HOW THE GAME IS PLAYED –

1. The players—a minimum of two—select the appropriate chapter. Without first looking at the questions, player number one picks a number from one to fifty. Player number two reads the corresponding question to player number one; player number one answers the question. Then the situation is reversed, and player number two becomes the question selector and answerer. When that sequence is completed, play moves to players three and four, and so on (or three and one if there are only three players). Each player in turn picks, answers, and then reads a question.

2. After the player has answered the question he or she has picked, other players may volunteer to answer that same question (without losing

their turn in the game). When this happens, lively discussion follows, and the fun has definitely begun.

3. Someone will keep a record of the numbers of the questions chosen, so that questions already dealt with will not be repeated.

4. When all of the questions are used up in a given chapter, the players may use another appropriate chapter. (See p. 13).

– RULES OF THE GAME –

1. When a number is picked, the player who picked that number **must** answer the question. He or she cannot say, "I want to pick a different question." A major part of the fun is the surprise and the random choice.

2. Each player must vow to be honest and to answer each question honestly and candidly.

3. Each player must allow the answerer to finish his answer without interruption.

4. If a player attacks an answerer for his or her answer, that player can be required to read out loud from page 123, "Are You Opinionated?"

–ANOTHER WAY TO PLAY THE GAME –

You may copy all of the questions from a given chapter onto separate pieces of paper (or even Xerox the questions and cut them up into question strips and place them in a bowl). You can then have each person pick a question and answer it. This is often more fun.

– CHAPTERS THAT CAN BE USED BY OVERLAP GROUPS –

Once you start playing the question game, you won't want to stop. But what happens when you run out of questions? For one thing, you can use certain chapters in addition to the one you chose for your special interest. When your special interest group is:

- Questions to Ask Someone You Are Dating, add: Questions to Ask in Mixed Company of Guys and Girls, Questions To Ask Anyone about Anything.
- Questions to Ask in Mixed Company of Guys and Girls, add: Questions to Ask Anyone about Anything.
- Questions to Ask Friends, add: Questions to

Ask in Mixed Company of Guys and Girls, Questions to Ask Anyone about Anything.

- Questions to Ask Parents, add: Questions to Ask Grandparents (modifying the wording of the questions), Questions to Ask Anyone about Anything.

- Questions for Parents to Ask Teens, add: Questions for Grandparents to Ask Teens, Questions to Ask Anyone about Anything.

- Questions to Ask Grandparents, add: Questions for Teens to Ask Parents (modifying the wording of the questions), Questions to Ask Anyone about Anything.

- Questions for Grandparents to Ask Teens, add: Questions for Parents to Ask Teens (modifying the wording of the questions), Questions to Ask Anyone about Anything.

- Questions to Ask Anyone about Anything, add: Your choice. It depends upon who anyone is. Use your own judgment.

– ADD TO THE GAME: MAKE UP YOUR OWN QUESTIONS –

If you really want to have fun, add to the game. Take advantage of the blank pages at the end of each chapter and make up some questions of your own.

At this point, either proceed to play a question

game of your choice, or turn to chapter ten (page 103). Beginning there, you'll find more hints on getting the greatest possible enrichment from your question-game experiences.

2

Questions to Ask in Mixed Company of Guys and Girls

1. When do you have more fun—when you're with your friends of the same sex, or when you're with your girlfriend or boyfriend? Explain.

2. If you are dating someone, do you think the guy should pay, or do you think you should go "dutch," with each person paying his or her own way? Why do you feel this way?

3. Name one thing about the opposite sex that you simply can't understand, or one thing that really bothers you. Explain your answer.

4. You are standing around with a group of your friends of the same sex; you notice someone across the room of the opposite sex and you

think that person is absolutely gorgeous, and he or she is, like you, with a group of people. Do you go right over and talk to the person you are attracted to, or do you talk to that person's friends first? Explain your answer.

5. Imagine you were going to an expensive college that you loved, and were doing well there. If you had a falling out with your parents and they refused to continue paying your tuition under any circumstances, what would you do?

6. Have you ever "used" someone of the opposite sex—either for money, favors, or sex? Confess it. Explain the circumstances and tell how you feel about it now. Has anyone ever "used" you? Tell what happened then and how you feel about it now.

7. If you were going out with someone you really loved, but that person didn't want to begin a sexual relationship with you, would you break up with that person because of his or her reluctance? If not, would you have sex with others? Explain your answer.

8. If someone murdered your mother or father, and was judged not guilty in a court of law, what would you do?

9. If you were engaged to marry someone, and that person became permanently paralyzed from the neck down, what would you do? What would you expect of your fiancé(e) if it happened to you?

10. If your entire family moved to the other side of the country, but gave you the choice of staying where you are now or going with them, and you were in love with someone, what would you do and why?

11. Do you think guys tend more toward forming long-lasting relationships than girls do? Or do you think it's the other way around? Explain your answer.

12. Do you think the root of many problems in America today is that more women have been leaving the home and entering the work force? Explain your answer.

13. What is the cruelest thing you've ever done to someone of the opposite sex? How do you feel about that now? What is the cruelest thing someone of the opposite sex has done to you? What have you learned from the experience?

14. Would you be willing to give up sex and/or any kissing or romantic involvement for one

year if (by some guaranteed miracle) that restraint would increase your I.Q. by one hundred points? Explain your answer.

15. What is the kindest or most generous thing you've ever done for someone? How did you feel after you did it? What is the kindest or most generous thing anyone has done for you? Which felt better? Explain your answer.

16. As a child, what was your favorite group game? Tell why.

17. List three personality traits and three physical traits that you like to find in the opposite sex.

18. On a scale of one to ten, how adventurous are you? How passionate? How good looking? How intelligent?

19. You already have a love interest, but also feel attracted to one of that person's friends. What do you do about it? Or, if you've actually been in that situation, what did you do?

20. Why do girls wear makeup when they are pretty without it? Do you think guys prefer girls to wear lots of makeup or little or no makeup? Explain your answer.

21. Why do so many guys really seem to prefer blondes? Is there a special kind of guy that most girls like? If so, why?

22. Do you view sex as something you do if you're deeply in love with someone, something you do only if you're married, or something that is purely physical? Explain your answer.

23. In general, are guys or girls more materialistic? Explain your answer.

24. How much about the relationship between you and the person you're dating do you tell your best friend? What kinds of details do you get into? Tell why.

25. What is the most foolish thing you've ever done for love? Tell why you did it and what you learned from the experience.

26. What is the biggest mistake you've made in your life so far? If you had it to do over again, what would you do this time? What did you learn from the mistake?

27. If someone you are dating couldn't stand your best friend, what would you do?

28. Would you, under *any* circumstances, pretend to be something you're not, just to win someone's heart? Explain your answer.

29. Would you leave the United States and live in Bangladesh for ten years for a million dollars? Assume you would be safe. You may not step foot out of that country for ten years and you would live modestly until the ten years are up. Then you would get the million. Explain your answer.

30. If there were a new law passed, and everyone had to marry someone of a different race, which race would you pick? Explain your answer.

31. Do you notice that your boyfriend (girlfriend) speaks to you and behaves toward you differently when he (she) is in front of his (her) friends than when the two of you are alone? How is the behavior different? Why do you think this happens? Are you guilty of this behavior? If so, explain why you engage in it.

32. If someone had a baby carriage and needed help to carry it down some stairs, would you stop and help that person, even if it meant you might miss your bus? What if that person begged you for help?

33. Did you ever do something embarrassing in front of a group of people so that everyone started laughing at you? Explain the situation. How did you feel? How did you handle it?

34. Is there really such a thing as date rape? Explain your answer.

35. Your father and your boyfriend (or mother and girlfriend) are trapped under a train. You can save only one. Who will it be? Explain your answer.

36. If you found out your boyfriend (girlfriend) had been seeing someone else behind your back—but you too had cheated, yet he (she) didn't know it—would you forgive him (her), or break up? What if you had not cheated? Under what circumstances would you forgive cheating?

37. What is the most common line guys use to get girls into bed? What is the most unusual you've ever heard? In your opinion, why is it that it is usually the guys who are giving the "lines" and working so hard to get girls into bed, and not the other way around?

38. If a person were in a group, and everyone was laughing at that person, and you knew why (his or her fly was open), would you tell that

person what was wrong, be quiet and mind your own business, or join the laughter? Explain your answer.

39. Do you believe in an afterlife? What happens after we die? What happens to those who do good or evil?

40. Suppose that you are to die right now, and that there is a God who really knows everything about your life. Would you be happy to face him or would you be afraid? Explain your answer.

41. If you could have a chance to talk to God tonight, and ask him any question, what would you ask? If God could tell you what to do with your life, would you want him to, and if he did, would you do the thing he prescribed, no matter what it was? Explain your answer.

42. What do you like best about your looks? What do you hate the most? What do you like best about your personality? What personality trait would you like to change? Explain your answer.

43. Which of the following is most important in someone you are going out with: looks, personality, dress, or the way the person kisses? Explain your answer.

44. What person are you closest to right now? What would you do if that person died?

45. Have you ever tried drugs? Which drug or drugs? And how did you feel the next day? Why don't (or do) you take drugs?

46. If you could get the best cosmetic surgeon to change your looks for free, so that you would be so stunning that people would stop and stare at you wherever you went, but the price would also be that you would not be recognized by anyone who knows you, and you would continually have to convince people that it was really you, would you do it? Explain your answer.

47. If you had to have one of the following, which would you pick: AIDS, cancer, or a bad heart that could go at any time? Explain your answer.

48. You are at a friend's party. You spill a drink on the rug, but no one sees you do it. Do you walk away and feign innocence, or politely confess and offer to pay for the cleaning?

49. If your friend's mother called your house to report that your friend didn't come home last night, and you knew that your friend was sleeping over with someone of the opposite sex, and would get in trouble if you told, what

would you do? The mother is hysterical out of fear that something terrible has happened. Explain your answer.

50. If you were in love with someone and engaged to be married, but that person did not approve of your career goal and insisted that you give it up if you wanted to marry him (her), what would you do? Explain your answer.

- MY OWN QUESTIONS -

3

----

*Questions to Ask Someone You Are Dating**

1. If you were to change your mind about someone you were dating, and wished to break up with that person, how would you go about it?

2. If you were in a relationship that began to bore you, would you end it or try to find ways to spice it up? Explain your answer.

3. If your girlfriend's (boyfriend's) best friend made a pass at you, and you were very attracted to that person, and if you believed no one would ever know if you two were together, how would you respond?

----

*Idea: Play this with your date person in a group—to put him or her at ease.

4. If your boyfriend (girlfriend) cheated on you, would you rather not know, and take the "what I don't know won't hurt me" attitude? Or would you rather know the truth? If your boyfriend (girlfriend) was honest with you, and told you the truth, would you forgive him (her)? Explain your answer.

5. If you were going out with someone and that person had to go away for six months, would you wait or would you go on to the next guy (girl)?

6. Have you ever been really hurt emotionally in a relationship? What happened? What do you feel would be the worst thing someone you are dating could do to you?

7. If you are a girl: Which of your father's traits do you admire, and look for in a future husband? If you are a guy: Which of your mother's traits would you look for in a future wife? What other qualities must the person you marry have? What are some qualities that you would *never* tolerate?

8. When you and I first met, exactly what was it about me that attracted you? Name one physical trait and one personality trait. Which was the more important to you?

9. If you had to decide whether I would lose 25 percent of my looks or 25 percent of my intelligence, but I must lose one or the other, which would you choose and why? Which would you choose for *yourself* and why?

10. If you could change one personality trait about me and one physical trait, what would those traits be and why would you choose them? Apply the question to yourself, too.

11. Would you rather date someone who is more intelligent than you or less intelligent? What about looks? Explain your answer.

12. What is the most romantic thing that you can imagine happening to you?

13. Which of your parents understands you best? Explain your answer.

14. If you could change one thing about your parents, what would it be? Discuss both mother and father—separately.

15. What is the cruelest thing your mother or father ever did to you? What is the best thing they ever did for you? Did you ever tell them how you felt about either of those instances?

Why or why not? If you did, what did you say
and how did they react?

16. How old were you when you first experienced
a feeling of love for someone of the opposite
sex? Exactly how did it feel?

17. There is someone you love deeply. Would you
marry that person if you would have to struggle for the rest of your lives because neither
one of you would ever make a lot of money
over all your years together? (This question
assumes that you'd have the option of marrying another person—someone you liked but
did not love, but with whom you knew you
would be very well off financially.) Explain
your answer.

18. As your dating relationship with someone
grows more serious, how would you react to
that person's continuing close friendship with
a third party of your own sex?

19. Do you think it's a good idea for people to
date if they work together or go to school together? Explain your answer.

20. Your girlfriend (boyfriend) decides to go away
for the weekend with her (his) friends. How
do you react?

21. Say that you were going out with and were deeply in love with a very rich person, but you suddenly discovered that that wealth was gained by ongoing illegal activities; when you confronted the person, you got the answer that "There's no way I'll ever get caught, and if I don't do it, someone else would anyway." Would your feelings for that person change? Explain your answer.

22. What is your greatest accomplishment so far?

23. In your opinion, how long does it take to fall in love? Do you ever want to get married? At what age? Would you like to have children? If so, how many? Explain your answer.

24. Do you think sex changes a relationship? Explain your answer. If possible, use yourself or a friend as an example.

25. If you saw someone being attacked and badly beaten, what would you do?

26. What is your most important goal in life? Why do you feel this way?

27. You receive bad news the night before an important exam. Do you simply not show up for the exam? Or do you take the exam without

studying? Or do you persevere and study in spite of the bad news? Explain your answer.

28. If you could live for a brief time with the guarantee of your safety while doing dangerous and daring things, what would you do and why?

29. Is honesty always the best policy, or is it okay to tell white lies? Explain your answer.

30. Paint a picture of yourself at thirty years old. What do you look like, where do you work, where do you live, how do you feel? Describe whatever aspects of your imagined life come to mind.

31. If your son or daughter were born mentally retarded, what would you do?

32. On a scale of one to ten, rate yourself in the following categories: kindness, reliability, honesty, affection, compassion, generosity, self-confidence. Justify your answers.

33. Do you prefer to be the center of attention, or to remain in the background? Explain your answer.

34. If you were taking a college admissions test and the questions were very difficult, and the person sitting next to you seemed to know all the answers and you could copy them without

getting caught, would you do it? Explain your answer.

35. What is the best compliment you've ever received from someone of the opposite sex? From someone of the same sex? Why did you feel so great about those compliments?

36. A roommate with whom you have never gotten along has gone away for the weekend. You stumble across two hundred dollars that he (she) had misplaced and has been searching for. Knowing that there is no way your roommate could ever find out if you kept the money, what would you do and why?

37. Do you ever pray? If so, when? Have you ever felt that God answered a prayer? Explain the situation. If you do not pray, explain why.

38. Which of your relatives do you admire most and why?

39. Have you ever in your life stolen anything? What and when? How did you feel afterward? What is the worst thing you have ever done (the thing you feel most guilty about)? What, if anything, did you do to make it right?

40. If you were drafted for war, and there was a safe escape provided so that you could get out

of being drafted, would you take that escape
or join the other draftees? Explain your answer.

41. If two people are dating and they start having
sex, is it possible for them to decide to stop
having sex but still continue the relationship?
Is it possible for a person who has had sex to
refrain from having sex in future relationships? Explain your answer.

42. On a scale of one to ten, rate each of the
following in importance for you in a dating relationship: physical attraction, emotional compatibility, intellectual compatibility, sexual
satisfaction, mutual respect and understanding,
fun and excitement. Now place the list in order of importance.

43. What would you advise your younger sister
regarding the right age to begin a sexual relationship? Why do you say this? How would
you advise your younger brother? Justify your
answers.

44. Did you ever have a girlfriend (boyfriend) that
dropped her (his) friends once the two of you
started going out? If so, how did you feel
about that and what did you do about it?
While you are going out with someone, do

you tend to drop your friends? If so, why? If not, why not?

45. What is the most embarrassing or outrageous thing you've ever done in a fit of jealousy?

46. Who is the favorite child in your family? How can you tell? How do you feel about the favoritism? Have you ever spoken to your parents about it? Why or why not?

47. We all have worries that drift through our minds during the course of a normal day. What are you worried about right now?

48. Is it important to you that you are liked or at least respected by your boyfriend's (girlfriend's) parents, or is their opinion of little value? Explain your answer.

49. If you could cure three injustices in the world, what would they be? Explain your answer.

50. Have you ever had a spiritual, mystical, or religious experience? What happened? In what way, if any, did it change your thinking or your life?

- MY OWN QUESTIONS -

– MY OWN QUESTIONS –

4

Questions to Ask Friends

1. If your friend had bad breath or body odor, would you tell her (him)? Why or why not? How would you approach the subject?

2. If your friend's boyfriend (girlfriend) asked you out, would you tell your friend? Why or why not?

3. Who was your best friend in elementary school? How did you become friends? Are you still friends? If not, what ended your friendship?

4. If you had an argument with your friend, and your friend was wrong but thought *you* were wrong, and the two of you were not talking, would you make the first move or wait for

your friend? What if your friend was stubborn, and you knew would never make the first move?

5. If your best friend started hanging out with someone else, and began telling you every time you called that she (he) was busy, would you confront your friend about this behavior, or would you just stop calling?

6. If your best friend started hanging out with someone who did drugs and otherwise behaved in ways you didn't approve of, and wanted to bring that person with you two when you went places, what would you do?

7. If you were in a situation with a friend where you two were not doing anything wrong, but the police were chasing you and caught your friend but not you, would you keep going or stay behind to help your friend?

8. If your friend was in a beauty or bodybuilding contest and you were one of the judges, and it came down to your vote deciding the contest, but your friend looked worse than the other contestants, would you vote for your friend or against her (him), knowing that your friend would never find out that it was your vote that decided the contest? Explain your answer.

9. What is the worst thing you've ever done to a friend? How did you feel about it afterward? What, if anything, did you do to make it up? What is the worst thing a friend has ever done to you?

10. If you and your friend are planning to go shopping together, but suddenly someone you are very attracted to calls, do you keep your date with your friend, knowing she (he) is counting on you, or do you go out with the caller? What if your friend was not simply looking forward to your company, but was very depressed and was counting on seeing you?

11. What is the most mischievous thing you've done, and what were the results of it?

12. What is the most embarrassing thing your mother or father ever did to you?

13. Think way back as far as you can. What is your first memory? How far can you go back?

14. What are the most important qualities in a friend? In your own opinion, are you a good friend?

15. If your friend were getting badly beaten in a fair fight, would you try to break up the fight

even though it might mean others would attack you, or would you stand by and wait it out?

16. Do you get embarrassed when you stumble or trip in front of a lot of people? When did that happen to you and how did you feel? In other words, tell about the time when you made the worst fool of yourself.

17. If your cousin was your age and you hadn't seen him (her) in ten years, and it turned out that he (she) was everything you ever wanted in a guy (girl) and the feelings were mutual, would you start a relationship with him (her?) Explain your answer.

18. If you had an opportunity to become rich and famous but the price would be a short life, would you do it? Or would you rather be poor and unknown, but live a long time?

19. You and your friend are at a club, and a gorgeous guy (girl) that everyone on campus (including you) has had their eye on shows up and puts a move on your friend. Are you happy for her (him) despite also feeling a bit sad you weren't the chosen one? Or do you wish something would go wrong?

20. If you had a choice, which would it be: a carefree life on this earth for eighty years and

complete annihilation after death, or eighty years of trouble, hardships, and toils in this life, but an eternal life of bliss after death?

21. If you were teaching a course, and your friend enrolled in that course, but no matter what he or she did that friend could not achieve a passing grade, would you pass the friend anyway, or fail him or her?

22. Do you believe that most people meet only one true friend in their lives? Explain your answer.

23. If you went to a friend's house and found a fifty-dollar bill carelessly thrown on the floor, and you so happened to be in desperate need of just that amount, what would you do and why?

24. Is it ever okay to date a friend's boyfriend (girlfriend), or should he (she) be strictly off limits?

25. Do you believe in God? Why or why not? What happens after we die?

26. If your friend was sick in the hospital and asked you to come visit on a Friday night, but you were invited to a party that you had been

longing to go to for months, what would you do and why?

27. If you'd just bought a gorgeous leather coat that you had not yet worn, and your friend had a very special date and begged you to let her (him) borrow it for just that one night, what would you do and why?

28. Under what circumstances, if any, would you allow a friend to borrow your car? What would you do if your friend borrowed your new car and totaled it? (You have no collision insurance on the car, and your friend has no money to pay for the loss.)

29. You are in love with the person your friend is dating, and neither party knows of your feelings. Would you tell your friend? Would you tell the person you're attracted to?

30. Is there any one thing a friend could do to you that, to your mind, would be unforgivable?

31. You and your friend have long planned a trip to the Bahamas. You are checking in at the gate, when she (he) is stopped for lack of a passport. You have yours and can still depart. Do you go or stay?

32. Starting with the most important, what are your three major goals for your life?

33. Choose your misfortune: either to be maimed for life so that your face was left appallingly ugly, though your body was unharmed, or to be paralyzed from the neck down but have a gorgeous face. What if, in the second case, the choice entailed paralysis from the waist down only?

34. What person do you love most in this world, and why?

35. Describe your first date. What did he (she) look like? How did you feel getting dressed for the date? Where did you go? What happened at the end of the evening?

36. Describe your first kiss. Were you nervous? Was it a pleasant or unpleasant experience?

37. If you were going out with a guy (girl) and he (she) had bought you a lot of very expensive gifts during the course of your relationship, but you had bought him (her) only modest gifts, would you return the gifts you'd received after breaking up, or keep them? What if he or she asked for them back? Explain your answer.

38. If your best friend told you a secret, and the secret turned out to be that he or she had committed a murder, what would you do?

39. They say everyone is prejudiced in some ways. Tell of a time when you caught yourself feeling or acting prejudiced. What did you learn from the experience? How would you define prejudice? In your opinion, what, if anything—at any time—might justify a prejudice?

40. What would you do if your friend was good friends with the person you were dating, and the two of them sometimes talked on the phone for hours at a clip?

41. How would you feel if your friend and your boyfriend (girlfriend) sometimes went places together (maybe shopping or to the movies) when you were not available—but they said they were going "just as friends"?

42. Do you think it's possible to have a strictly platonic friendship (a brother-sister type of relationship) with the opposite sex? Give an example to back up your answer.

43. Have you ever felt the urge to slap or even punch someone in the face, but held back? What exactly stopped you from lashing out?

Looking back, are you now glad or sorry that you used restraint?

44. Tell of a time when you cried, or almost cried, in front of someone and were very embarrassed about your show of emotion.

45. If you and your friend were competing for the same spot on the team, and—by cheating—your friend got it, what would you do?

46. Did you ever think of committing suicide? What was happening in your life at the time? How close did you get to doing it and what thoughts stopped you?

47. Think back. What was your happiest birthday? Tell about it.

48. Your friend is extremely good-looking, and your boyfriend (girlfriend) has commented on her (his) appearance more than once. Do you slowly weed her (him) out of your social plans that involve your boyfriend (girlfriend), or do you simply agree that she (he) is striking, and leave it at that?

49. Who was your all-time favorite teacher, and why? Describe the worst teacher you've ever had. Have you ever been a teacher's pet?

50. Have you ever gotten a low or failing mark because the teacher was unfair? Explain. What, if anything, did you do about it?

- MY OWN QUESTIONS -

- MY OWN QUESTIONS -

5

Questions to Ask Parents

---

1. How did you two meet, and how long after that did you fall in love? How did you know you were in love?

2. If money had been no object, how many children would you have had?

3. If you couldn't have children, would you have adopted a child? Why?

4. If I had never been born, how would your lives have been different?

5. If you could somehow pick my future career, what would it be? Why?

6. If you had to choose between your child's marrying a starving artist with whom she (he) was madly in love, or a wealthy doctor with whom she (he) would have mediocre satisfaction, which would you select? Explain your answer.

7. What is the biggest mistake you made in your life? If you had that situation to do over again, what would you do differently?

8. When in your life were you most afraid? What thoughts went through your mind? How did it all turn out?

9. At this point in your life, what goals do you hope to achieve?

10. If you had a choice of either extending your life by ten years (you don't know when you will die) or doubling your intelligence, which would you choose? Explain your answer.

11. If you were offered a stipend of one hundred thousand dollars a year and a full scholarship to become qualified in any career you wanted, which career would you choose? Explain your answer.

12. If I were accused of a crime you were sure I did not commit, and was found guilty but was

out on bail, would you help me to escape to another country, or would you encourage me to do my time? Explain your answer.

13. When were you most worried about me? What were your greatest fears?

14. Give an example of when you were embarrassed by one or both of your parents.

15. In what ways do you find yourself treating your children as your parents treated you—ways you'd sworn to yourself you would avoid?

16. Did you ever do or say something to me that you were sorry about, and wanted to apologize for, but didn't? What was it and what kept you from apologizing?

17. So far, when were you most proud of me and happy to have me as your child?

18. What positive trait do I possess that neither you nor Dad (Mom) possesses?

19. If you were allowed to give me only three rules for a happy life, what would those rules be?

20. If I came home pregnant (or if I got a girl pregnant), would you want me to confide in

you? Or would you rather I secretly handled the problem on my own? If I confided in you, what advice would you give me?

21. Which are most important to you: financial security, self-esteem, or faith in God? Explain your priorities.

22. What would you do to help me if you found out I was doing drugs?

23. In what ways were your parents a positive influence on how you turned out as a person? If your parents were indifferent to you, do you think you would have been as successful as you are today? Explain your answer.

24. You must choose which is the healther scenario: the way you have raised your own children, or the way your parents have raised you. Explain your answer.

25. You must suffer one of two consequences: have your child marry a pauper, or have your child marry a wealthy spouse who would take wonderful care of him or her but who you know is a corrupt man without a conscience. Explain your answer.

26. Have I ever embarrassed you? Give an example.

27. Mom, what went through your mind when you found out you were pregnant with me? What did you think when you first saw me? When you were expecting, did you hope for a boy or a girl? How did I behave the first week I was home? (Ask your father an adapted version of this question.)

28. On a scale of one to ten, rate yourself as a parent. What trait do you wish you had more of in order to be a better parent? What was the hardest thing you had to do as a parent, yet the right thing?

29. What was your biggest mistake as a parent?

30. What was your most severe punishment as a child or a teenager?

31. When your mother was yelling at you, did the thought to say "I hate you" ever go through your mind? Exactly why did you feel that way at the moment?

32. Did you ever try drugs? If so, why did you choose not to continue taking them? If not, were you ever tempted and what made you decide to say no?

33. If I moved in with my boyfriend (girlfriend) at the age of eighteen, what would you do? What

would you do if I dropped out of high school and got a menial job?

34. What was the most difficult obstacle that you've had to overcome in your life?

35. Compare your high school to mine. How was it different, and how was it the same? What was your favorite subject? How popular were you in high school?

36. When you were a teen, did you ever feel ugly or inferior in any way? Explain your answer.

37. Did your parents ever criticize the way you dressed or wore your hair when you were a teenager? Give examples. How did you respond to your parents on those issues?

38. When you were younger, you probably planned your life in at least certain particulars. How many of your plans came to be and how many didn't? Were any of those expectations exceeded?

39. What is the purpose of a curfew?

40. Did you ever have a bad fight with another child or teen where you came home with some serious cuts and bruises? How did your parents react when they saw your condition?

41. Should parents discuss sex with their children? What is a good age to start? Do you think discussions promote sexual activity, prevent sexual activity, or are simply informative? Explain your answer.

42. What was your favorite sport or hobby when you were a teen? Why?

43. Is it possible for a parent to be both parent and friend to a teen, or must one role prevail over the other? Explain your answer.

44. Are you happy with your job? What is your greatest aggravation at work? What do you like most about your job?

45. When you come home from work, how long does it take you to unwind? How do you feel when you see a mess in the house or hear loud music?

46. What was your first job? How old were you? How did you feel about the job?

47. If you found my diary, would you read it? Did your parents ever read your diary?

48. What would you think if I wanted to marry someone twice my age?

49. Which of my friends did or do you like the best and which did or do you like least—and why? When you were a teenager, did you have any friends that your parents disliked?

50. Looking back, did your friends have a major influence on your behavior? Did you have a major influence on the behavior of any of your friends? Explain your answers.

- MY OWN QUESTIONS -

6

Questions for Parents to Ask Teens

1. If we were both killed in a plane crash, with whom would you want to live? Why?

2. If you could decide where we lived, and money was no object, where would you want to live? Why?

3. If you could change one thing about your looks, what would it be? Explain your answer.

4. If you could magically become either 30 percent more intelligent or 30 percent better looking, which would you choose? Explain your answer.

5. What do you hope to be doing ten years from now?

6. Picture me as a teenager. How do you think I behaved when I went out with my friends? What was my attitude toward the opposite sex?

7. If you could make up three rules that all parents must obey, what would they be? (These must be serious rules—in other words, don't say "Parents must give their teens all the money they want.")

8. Which of your personality traits do you think you've inherited—through genetics or influence—from your mother, and which do you get from your father? Which traits do you have that neither one of us possesses?

9. What was the saddest moment of your life? Why?

10. If you found out that *your* teenager was having sex, how would you react?

11. Did you ever say to yourself about your parent, "She (he) doesn't love me"? What was going on at that time?

12. At what age do you want to get married? How many children do you want to have, and at what age do you want to have them?

13. If you had an early curfew but wanted to go to a club far away, and you knew you wouldn't be home before 3:00, would you ask your parents if you could stay out later? Or would you ask permission to stay over at the house of someone you know has a later curfew? Explain your answer.

14. If you could turn back the clock and correct one mistake in your life, what would that be? Explain your answer.

15. Did I ever wear or do anything that embarrassed you? Exactly what went through your mind at that moment?

16. How do you feel when I scream at you? What goes through your mind?

17. Think back to your childhood. What is your happiest memory?

18. When you were a child, did you ever do something that you were afraid to tell me about because you feared a punishment? Did I ever find out? If not, tell me now.

19. Sometimes children or teens become so angry with parents that they at least *think* "I hate you." Have you ever experienced that impulse? Explain the circumstances.

20. Did you ever like someone romantically who did not like you in the same way? How did you deal with it?

21. What is the best thing that you like about me (us) as a parent (parents)?

22. Do you ever feel that no one understands you? Who understands you best at this point in your life? How do you know that?

23. Did you ever wish you'd never been born? What was happening at the time? How long did it take for that feeling to pass?

24. How do you think you would have turned out if we'd let you do anything you wanted once you turned thirteen?

25. In your opinion, how much of the way one turns out is one's own fault, and how much is the fault of the parent? Explain your answer.

26. When you are the parent of a teenager, what will you do differently from the way I (we) have treated you? What will you do the same?

27. When you have children, if you could choose between having a child exactly like yourself and having one who is the opposite of you in

every way, which would be your choice and why?

28. Would you be happy living basically the same life that your parents live? If not, in what ways would you like your life to be different?

29. What, in your opinion, is the most difficult part of being a parent?

30. If you were pregnant (or if you got a girl pregnant) would you confide in your parents? Which of us would you tell first?

31. Parents want teens to be honest, yet they make it impossible sometimes. What are some of the reasons teens lie to parents, and how do you think parents can change so that teens can be more honest with them?

32. Do you ever feel neglected by either of your parents?

33. Were you ever ashamed of either of your parents? Describe the circumstances. Did you feel guilty about being ashamed?

34. Do you ever view your parents as friends? If they weren't your parents, would you like them? Explain your answer.

35. What family function do you most enjoy? Which do you most dread? Why?

36. Parents are sometimes unfair and sometimes unwittingly treat children cruelly. When was I (when were we) most unfair or cruel to you? What thoughts went through your mind at the time? How would you have wanted to be treated in that situation?

37. What are the best parts of being a teenager? What are the most difficult?

38. If you could remain a teenager for the rest of your life, would you do so? Why or why not?

39. When you really want your parents to buy you something, such as a television, stereo, or an item of clothing, is it difficult or easy? What about persuading them to raise your curfew or to withdraw a punishment?

40. If you could have been born in a different time in history, what time would you choose, and why?

41. In your opinion, why are parents sometimes short-tempered or grouchy?

42. Did you ever look at me and feel sorry for me? What was the situation?

43. What worries go through your mind during a typical day? For example, exactly what are you worried about right now?

44. Think back. How did you feel on your first day of school?

45. Did the thought of suicide ever pass through your mind? What was going on in your life at the time? What was it that stopped you from doing it?

46. Educate me. Why do teenagers talk on the phone so much? Give me typical examples of what subjects you cover in a conversation with your best friend and with someone you are going out with.

47. Help me. As you say, "I don't know what's happening." In your estimation, what percent of teenagers at each of these ages—fourteen, fifteen, sixteen, seventeen, and eighteen—are having sex? In your opinion, what is the ideal age to start having sex?

48. Did you ever seriously consider running away from home? What was happening at the time? Why did you decide not to run away?

49. What is the dream you most dearly hope to fulfill in your lifetime?

50. If you and I could make a deal and I would be willing to change my behavior toward you in one way, what would you be willing to change in exchange so that the deal would be fair to both of us?

– MY OWN QUESTIONS –

7

Questions to Ask Grandparents

1. Have times changed for the better or for the worse? What opportunities are available to young people today that weren't available when you were a teenager?

2. If you were stranded on an island and could have only one book to read, which book would that be, and why?

3. What is the wildest thing you've done in your life, and what were the consequences?

4. How many people did you date before you met Grandpa (Grandma)? Was Grandpa (Grandma) the first person you fell in love with? If not, why didn't you marry that other person?

5. Do you believe that everything that happens is destiny? Explain your answer.

6. What was your economic situation when you were a teenager? Did you have to put cardboard in the soles of your shoes? Looking back, were you happy or sad as a teenager?

7. Have you accomplished everything you most wanted to accomplish in life, or are there still things you're trying to achieve?

8. How did you feel about school when you were a teenager?

9. How does it feel to be your age? Have you become more easygoing as the years have gone by, or less so? What are things that used to bother you, but don't anymore? Do any things bother you now that didn't bother you before?

10. When my mother (father) was a teenager, did you ever blame her (him) for something she (he) didn't do, and find out later that you were wrong?

11. If you could have stopped the clock at any specific age, what age would that be? Explain your answer.

12. How old were you when you had your first boyfriend (girlfriend)? What did your parents have to say about it?

13. Why do you (or do you not) go to church (or synagogue or other place of worship)?

14. What is the most devilish thing my mother (father) ever did when she (he) was a teenager? What was her (his) punishment?

15. When my mother (father) was a teenager, did you ever worry that she (he) would turn out to be a bum or a loser? What did you do to keep her (him) on track? What was your favorite lecture to my mother (father), and now that she (he) is grown, how successful do you think you were as a parent?

16. What was my mother's (father's) curfew at my age? Did she (he) ever come home late and get punished?

17. Did my mother (father) ever go out with anyone you didn't care for? Why did you feel that way? What did you do about it?

18. Were you stricter with my mother (father) than she (he) is with me, or were you less strict? Give me an example.

19. What did you have to nag my mother (father) about over and over again?

20. What do you like best about me? Why?

21. In what ways do I take after you? In what ways do I take after my mother (father)? In what ways am I very different from my mother (father)?

22. In your opinion, what careers would be good choices for me? Why?

23. Do you see a lot of yourself in your own children? In what ways?

24. When you were a teenager, who was your favorite singer? What type of music did you like to listen to and dance to? What is your favorite music today?

25. Where did you meet Grandma (Grandpa) and how did you start dating?

26. How did Grandpa ask you to marry him? (How did you ask Grandma to marry you?) Who was more in love, you or Grandpa (Grandma)? How did your love change over the years?

27. What is the most important thing about a marriage?

28. What was your first paying job? How old were you? How much did you make? How long were the hours? Did you like it or hate it? Why?

29. In your opinion, which is more important: to like your job or to get a high salary? Explain your answer.

30. Name three books that I as a young adult should read, and tell me why I should read them.

31. In your opinion, what builds "character" and why?

32. In what ways would you like me to follow in your footsteps? What mistakes did you make that you would like to see me avoid?

33. When you were a teenager, what major problems did you have with boys or girls?

34. When you were a teenager, what did you hate most about your looks and wish you could change, and what did you like most about your looks? Explain your answers.

35. Do you have any friends now? How many? Who is your best friend? Why is that person your best friend?

36. Do you have any secrets that to this day no one knows, or that maybe only one or two people know? Would you ever tell anyone?

37. What do you think happens after death? Are you more afraid to die now than when you were a teenager, or less afraid? Explain your answer.

38. What is the most difficult obstacle you've had to overcome in your life? Did it, in the long run, make you a stronger person? How?

39. If you had a choice, would you rather be a teenager now, or when you were a teenager? Explain your answer.

40. When my mother (father) was a teenager, did you talk to her (him) about sex? If not, where did she (he) learn the facts of life?

41. Was my mother (father) a good student? What was her (his) best subject?

42. Looking back, what was the most exciting moment of your life?

43. In the long run, what is most important in life?

44. Do you feel important in your children's lives, or do you feel left out? Explain your answer.

45. Looking back, what mistakes do you feel you made in raising my mother (father)? How would you do things differently if you had them to do over again? Have you been able to forgive yourself for the mistakes you perceive, or do you still blame yourself?

46. If it could have been worked out, which career do you wish you had pursued? Why didn't you pursue it? In the big picture, how important is the loss?

47. Do you ever feel sad or depressed? When? Exactly what goes through your mind? How do you cheer yourself up?

48. Do you ever think about your friends from the olden days? Do you still keep in touch with any friends you had when you were a teenager?

49. Is it true that when you were a teenager, people didn't have to lock their doors when they

went out? Where did you live and what was
the neighborhood like?

50. In your lifetime, which invention has most im-
pressed you?

– MY OWN QUESTIONS –

- MY OWN QUESTIONS -

8

Questions for Grandparents to Ask Teens

---

1. If today I were suddenly turned back into a teenager, and I had to face the world, what advice would you give me about the opposite sex?

2. Do you feel that your parents understand you? Why or why not?

3. If you had to live in a house that was ten degrees too hot or ten degrees too cold, which would you choose?

4. When I ask this question, I want you to say the first thing that comes into your mind: If someone were to write a book about your life, what would the title be?

5. Even though I'm not young, I still want to have fun. Tell me three things I can do.

6. Do I look like a grandmother (grandfather)? What does a "typical" grandparent look like?

7. Picture yourself as a grandparent: What do you look like?

8. Do you think I should try to find ways to make myself look younger, or would you rather that I stay the way I am? If I wanted to look younger, what would you suggest?

9. What traits do you see in me that you also see in your mother (father)?

10. What personality traits do you look for in a boyfriend (girlfriend)? Why?

11. Which television or movie personality most resembles your physical ideal in someone of the opposite sex?

12. Which is more important to you: love, or financial security? If you fell in love with a poor person, and at the same time were mildly attracted to a wealthy person who wanted to marry you, what would you do? Explain your answer.

13. When you look at older people, do you ever feel sorry for them? If not, what do you feel and think?

14. Can you picture me as mother (father) to your mother (father) when she (he) was your age? What kind of a parent do you think I was then? In all honesty, can you think of something I should have done differently?

15. Everyone makes mistakes. What is the biggest mistake you've made so far? When did you realize your mistake? If you can't think of a big mistake, what are some small ones?

16. Whom do you trust most in this world? Talk about it.

17. Whom do you respect most in this world and why?

18. If you could choose how long you will live, what age would you pick and why?

19. Picture yourself when you are my age. How will you feel? What will be your goal in life?

20. What do you wish you could become—but may doubt that you have the ability to achieve? In other words, tell me your wildest

dream for your life—something you really
want to do.

21. If a condom company were to pay you five
hundred dollars to go on a national talk show
and make a one-sentence statement about the
superiority of their product, would you do it?
The catch is, you would have to blurt this out
at some point during the show, even though
the topic would have nothing to do with con-
doms. In addition, under no conditions would
you be allowed to tell the producers of the
show or the audience that you were being paid
by the company to push their product. If you
wouldn't do it for five hundred dollars, would
you do it for a thousand? If not, what would
your price be? What are some other ways in
which you would be willing to make a fool of
yourself for money?

22. If your parents could afford to send you to any
college in the world, where would you go?

23. If given a choice of one or the other, which
would you choose: endless wealth but little
success, or little wealth but extreme success.

24. As you see it, at what age did you cease being
a child, and begin being a young adult? How
did you know?

25. Have you ever defended someone who was being unfairly treated? What were the circumstances, and why did you help that person?

26. What are some of the things you can't talk about to your parents without getting into an argument?

27. On a scale of one to ten, how popular are you among your friends? What does it take to be popular these days?

28. In most high schools, there are different types of teenagers that hang out in cliques. What are the different groups in your school? Which, if any, group do you associate with?

29. I know things have changed drastically since my day, especially when it comes to teen sex. I'm curious. How do other teens react to someone who is eighteen years old, good-looking, lots of fun, but insists upon remaining a virgin?

30. In your opinion, what three things in life are more important than money?

31. If your house were on fire and you had a chance to save only one item, what would it be?

32. If your house were burning and your pet were still in it, but by going back, you would only have a fifty-fifty chance of surviving, what would you do?

33. Different things annoy different people. Some hate eating noises, others hate gum snapping. What annoys you?

34. What is the most generous thing you've ever done and exactly how did you feel afterward?

35. If you had the chance to become the president of the United States, would you take the job? Why or why not?

36. Out of the three professions: doctor, lawyer, and teacher, which do you respect the most? Explain your answer.

37. Many people believe that each person was born for a reason, or put on this earth to accomplish a "job" in life. Reach deep into yourself and tell me what you think your "job" in life will be. Why do you say this?

38. In what ways am I different from other grandparents, and in what ways am I the same?

39. What do you like best about me? Why?

40. Most violent crimes and most drug abuse are committed by people under forty. Why do you think this is so?

41. Do you ever feel that your parents favor one of your brothers or sisters over you? If so, whom do they favor and how can you tell? Have you ever talked about this with your parents? (Or, to an only child: Has your parent ever compared you to anyone unfavorably?)

42. If I asked you to go with me to the movies, would you be too embarrassed to be seen in the movie theater with your grandparent, or would you go? If you wouldn't go to the movies with me, where could we go together with no embarrassment to you?

43. If I were gone, what would you miss most about me?

44. Which is more important for grandparents to do: cook good meals, give out wise advice, or present a good spiritual or religious example?

45. Tell me a secret: Do you like your mother's cooking? Which is your favorite dinner and which do you like the least?

46. What was the proudest moment of your life? Why?

47. Regarding schoolwork, are you the type of student who can get away with not reading all the required books and still get a good grade? If so, do you take advantage of that ability, or do you read the required material anyway? Explain your answer.

48. If the country were at war and it desperately needed volunteers to fight to save it, would you volunteer? Explain your position.

49. What is the most important thing in your life right now? Why?

50. Go back in time: What is your happiest childhood memory with your mother (father)?

– MY OWN QUESTIONS –

9

Questions to Ask Anyone about Anything

---

1. Did you ever have the experience of going out with someone you were attracted to, only to find that you couldn't stand the way that person ate or danced or looked in a certain item of clothing, or some such thing? Was that turnoff enough to cause you to end your relationship?

2. If without effort you could be given the ability to speak three foreign languages, which languages would you choose? Why?

3. If you could immediately, magically possess any of the following attainments, which would you choose: a doctor's degree in an area of your interest, fame as a television personality,

or a successful and exciting business of your choice? Explain your answer.

4. If you won a contest offering these prizes, which would you select if you could choose any one: first-class trip around the world for three months, with paid time off from work; the car of your dreams; or the guarantee of spending twenty-four hours with any celebrity—Hollywood, political, or other?

5. If you had to do one of the following, which would you choose: jump out of a plane in a parachute, walk across a pit of deadly snakes on a thin plank in shorts and bare feet, or swim through waters in which a shark has been spotted recently?

6. What is the most important item you've lost and never found? How many times did you go back and look in the same place for that item, even though you knew you had looked there before? Why did you keep looking in that same place?

7. In your opinion, out of one hundred people, how many would return the money in a wallet (the sum of one thousand dollars) if they found the wallet with a name, address, and telephone number? What would you do?

8. If you could fly through the air like a bird, but would attract great attention in doing so, on what occasions, if any, would you take advantage of your ability?

9. Do you believe in a supreme being? If not, how do you explain creation? How do you explain evil?

10. If someone you really loved were dying, and the only way that person could live would be by your sacrificing your life, would you do it? For whom, if anyone, would you make this sacrifice?

11. For a hundred thousand dollars, would you keep a hundred cats in your apartment for a year, under the condition that they must all be alive and healthy at the end of the year? Keep in mind that you would not be paid a cent if even one cat were in ill health.

12. For a hundred thousand dollars, would you agree to be homeless for one year, under the condition that you would be paid only at the end of the year? If you wouldn't do it for a hundred thousand dollars, for what price, if any, would you do it?

13. Do you believe in the law of karma (what goes around comes around, or, your deeds return

upon you, sooner or later)? Justify your answer.

14. How do you feel about interracial marriage? Would you marry someone of another race? Explain your position.

15. If you could take three lovers at the same time and there would be no way they could find out about one another, would you do it? Explain your answer.

16. If your house burned to the ground with all of your earthly possessions, where would you live? What steps would you take to get your life back in order?

17. If you were fired from your job tomorrow, when and where would you begin to look for another job? How could you turn being fired into an advantage—or could you?

18. If you found a newborn baby at your doorstep, with a note begging you not to give it up to the authorities, but to take care of it for three months with the promise that the mother would return after that time, what would you do? Why?

19. Do you like ball sports, such as tennis, basketball, volleyball, handball, golf? Why or why not?

20. If you had an opportunity, through expert instruction, to become accomplished in horsemanship, mountaineering, the martial arts, piloting, parachute jumping, deep sea diving, or hunting, which would you choose?

21. Brag about yourself: What are your three greatest virtues? Humble yourself: What are your three greatest faults? What, if anything, are you doing to correct the faults?

22. Under what circumstances, if any, would you seek the help of a psychiatrist or a psychoanalyst? In your opinion, what percent of the population would benefit from such therapy?

23. Would you ever sign a prenuptial agreement, or ask anyone else to do so? Explain your position.

24. Confess it: What is the most shameful thing you've ever done? Have you forgiven yourself yet? Why or why not?

25. If you had to give up one of the following for a year, which would you choose: television, music, all sports and athletic activities, reading of anything at all, laughing or smiling, drinking of any alcoholic beverage, any sweetened food, or talking on the telephone?

26. How much money would you have to earn a year in order to be perfectly content? Explain your answer.

27. Choose which the following experiences with nature you would most like to have, and give the reasons for your choice: a trek through a lush tropical jungle, a trip down the Nile River in an open boat, a climb to the top of Mount Everest, a trip down the Snake River on a rubber raft, a ride to the bottom of the Grand Canyon on a mule, or a ride through the Sahara Desert on the back of a camel. Assume that your life and health will be preserved no matter which you choose.

28. Look back at your life and think of a time when you made a decision not to do something that was tempting, but that you felt in your "gut" was wrong. At the time you thought you might be giving something up, but, unable to ignore your inner voice, you did in fact do "the right thing." Tell why, looking back now, you realize it was a good thing you listened to your "gut."

29. How many hours a week do you spend watching television? List three things you wish you had time to do. What would happen if you gave your television time to those things?

How would you feel about yourself and your
life? Why?

30. Which of these qualities do you admire most
in a person: loyalty, courage, integrity, disci-
pline, or altruism (genuine love and generosity
toward others)? Which do you possess? Name
first the quality you possess in greater measure
than any of the others.

31. If you had an opportunity to get straight A's in
one of the top universities in the country, and
were able to do so without ever reading a book
or studying for a test (you could somehow
guess exactly what the teacher wanted to
hear), would you do it? Realize that part of the
deal would be that you would not be allowed
to read any books, even if you wanted to. (The
alternative would be to go to that same school,
read the books, and take your chances.)

32. If you were a multimillionaire, and had mil-
lions to donate to helping others, whom would
you help and why?

33. Which of the following traits apply to you:
charming, intellectual, sensitive, productive,
sensual, romantic, logical, practical? Add three
other traits that also apply to you.

34. If you had the power to shoot a thought into another person's mind, and make that person call you on the telephone right now, whom would you have call you and why?

35. Which public figure do you most dislike or even despise? Explain your answer.

36. Whom do you think is the least talented movie or television star and what goes through your mind when you see or hear of that person?

37. They say fame is difficult to handle. What position of fame could you handle? What position of fame could you not handle? Explain your position.

38. If you had the power to plug your mind into any moment, hour, day, week, month, or year in the future and see a movie of exactly what will happen at that time, how would you use your power?

39. Should people live together before they marry? Explain your position.

40. If your future spouse proposed that the two of you agree that once in a while it's okay to have an extramarital "event" (a fling, not a drawn-out affair) would you agree? Explain your reasoning.

41. One of these two consequences must befall you; you must choose which: You are driving drunk and crash head-on into another automobile and a) you are paralyzed for life; b) the person you hit is paralyzed for life. Explain your choice.

42. If you killed someone while driving drunk, would you ever forgive yourself? If so, how long do you think it would take? What steps, if any, would you take to make it up to the family of the person you killed?

43. Would you rather have two children of your own who would give you continual heartache, or two adopted children who would give you great joy? Explain your answer.

44. How much does it bother you when something negative is said about you, when that something is totally untrue? To what extent would you go to prove your innocence? (You will be in no legal trouble, nor will your job be jeopardized if you let the lie rest.)

45. If you gave your telephone number to someone, but later thought better of it and that person called you for a date, would you honestly tell him (her) that you don't want to go out? Or would you make an excuse and let that person continue to call? When, if ever,

would you tell the truth? If the situation were reversed, how would you wish to be treated?

46. When is the last time you told a major lie? In what situations, if any, is prevarication excusable?

47. If you could live for one year as a member of the opposite sex, would you do it? Would you be willing to live for one year as a person of another race? If so, which race would you choose? Why?

48. If you could live for five hundred years, but stop aging at the age of fifty (so that you would look and feel fifty for the last 450 years of your life), would you do it? Assume that once you made your decision, you would not be able to die before your five hundredth birthday. Explain your answer.

49. Which of the following powers would you choose if you could have only one: the power to read people's thoughts, the power to kill people by just wishing them dead, or the power to make people love you by wishing it? Explain your answer.

50. Some people are of the opinion that drugs and alcohol are exactly the same. State your position on this subject.

– MY OWN QUESTIONS –

10

Coping with the Answers

If you've already played the question game, you'll know exactly what I'm talking about in this last chapter. If you haven't, the chapter will serve to alert you to what to expect, and will possibly help you to avoid getting into arguments, rejecting people because their views differ from your own, or becomming confused because you now realize that your values are in conflict with others— sometimes people who are important in your life.

The question game is a learning experience. At times, you'll learn that others share your ideas and opinions. When your own views are confirmed in this way, naturally you'll be delighted. You may discover that your ideas and values are closely aligned with those of certain other people; that your friendship has an even broader base than you had supposed.

Other times, however, you'll learn that some people disagree with you one hundred percent. When this happens, it may make you feel uncomfortable, threatened, or even angry—especially if the player who expresses the opposite opinion is someone close to you.

When you discover that others do not share your values, you may be tempted to argue, name call, or even reject the person outright. Don't fall into that trap. Instead, use self-control. You won't regret this exercise in restraint, because if you hold off judgment, and give your mind time to process the information, you may realize that the differences in your thinking do not merit severing the relationship. You may realize that it isn't necessary for you to agree on every point with even your closest friends or relatives. You may decide to live and let live in the area of disagreement.

On the other hand, after thinking it over, you may decide that your values differ so much that you no longer feel comfortable maintaining a relationship with this person. If this happens, all well and good. But make sure it's a carefully thought out decision, and not a snap judgment.

Other times, the game is neither reinforcing nor threatening; it is revelatory. It helps you to understand on a deeper level someone you have known for a long time. This insight is bound to improve your relationship with that person.

But what about playing the game with relatives? In the case of parents and grandparents, you need not worry about the learning of conflicting values: Chances are, if you are at odds in your values, you already know it—and probably already argue about those differences. The questions in the parent and grandparent chapters are designed to help these two groups to better understand you, and you them. The end result of playing the game with these loved ones will be a closer bond and a deeper and more mutual understanding.

In the following paragraphs, one question from each chapter is discussed in terms of three possible answers. The goal is to help you to see that people have different ways of looking at things, and to help you to build up a tolerance toward opposing points of view.

Remember, by accepting the right of other people to have an opposing point of view, you are not saying that you agree with that point of view. In fact, in offering that acceptance you are reaffirming your *own* right to have a different, and yet completely valid, opinion.

Question from Chapter Two:
Mixed Company of Guys and Girls

8. If someone murdered your mother or father, and was judged not guilty in a court of law, what would you do?

Answer 1. "I would either hire a hit man to kill that person, or I would do it myself.

way. The law is in favor of the crimi-
nals. You have to do things yourself."

Answer 2. "I would leave it alone. That person
will get what's coming to him in life.
What goes around comes around.
Anyway, I wouldn't want to become a
criminal myself."

Answer 3. "God will take care of it. The Bible
says, 'Vengeance is mine saith the
Lord. I will repay.' "

As you can see, each answer represents a different philosophy. Answerer number one, who would
hire a hit man or would himself kill the murderer,
believes in taking the law into his own hands when
he perceives that justice would not otherwise be
served. Answerer number two has faith in the law
of the universe, and believes that farther up the
road, somehow, people stumble into the punishment they deserve. In addition, answerer number
two thinks it's wrong to break the law under any
circumstances. Answerer number three has a simple faith in a just God.

Your reaction to answerers number one, two, and
three will of course depend upon your philosophy.
If your thinking is more like that of answerer
number one, and if you don't believe in karma
(what goes around comes around) or in a just God

who rights all wrongs, and if you feel that under certain circumstances, the law must be broken, you may become very angry. You may retort by saying:

"What a sucker you are. You mean you would just let someone get away with doing anything to you and your family, in the foolish belief that somehow, by magic, they'll get punished? You mean to tell me you would worry about the law even if your parents were killed?"

But remember this: By now, the other two answerers would surely feel just as furious about your position as you feel about theirs. They might come back at you with:

"Oh, that's great. You would just hit them off, like the Mafia. If everyone did that, people would be killing one another for every which reason and our society would be in complete chaos. You have to be civilized."

or

"If you had faith in God, you wouldn't think that way. Your problem is, you're an atheist. You need to get some religion."

The arguments could be endless. So what should you do? If you hear an answer that offends you and you find yourself becoming furious, acknowledge what you are feeling—and then instead of reacting, catch your anger like a rubber ball. Look at it, and refuse to react. That will give you time to think about the answer and your reaction to it. Do that and you'll realize that the speaker has a right to his or her opinion, and you'll feel less threatened—especially when you remind yourself that no one is truly expecting you to change your opinion.

It's fine to disagree. But when beliefs are firmly held, "agreeing to disagree" is where it should end. There's no reason completely to lose respect for someone, or to call a person names, even if that person's philosophy is diametrically opposed to your own. In fact, if you listen, you may even see that others have some valid points. And *listening doesn't mean you have to change your mind.*

Question from Chapter Three:
Someone You Are Dating

34. If you were taking a college admissions test and the questions were very difficult, and the person sitting next to you seemed to know all the answers and you could copy them without getting caught, would you do it? Explain your answer.

Answer 1. "Never. Cheating is wrong. I would lose respect for myself if I cheated. I'll take my chances and get what I get.

At least I know it represented the real me and not someone else."

Answer 2. "Probably I wouldn't copy off him, because he may be breezing through but be a real dummy. But if I knew for sure that his answers were right and I wouldn't get caught, I would copy. In a situation, you do what you have to do to get ahead."

Answer 3. "I would copy. Why not? Everybody else does it. The whole world is cheating in one way or another. If I have a chance, lucky me. If I'm a goody-goody, and a fool, I'll be the only one and I'll be left behind."

Each answer represents a different code of ethics or value system. Answer number one implies high integrity linked to self-esteem. This person cannot cheat; she believes that cheating means making a statement about herself—that she is a fraud. Rather than risk loss of self-respect, she would do the best she could on the test, unaided.

If a guy hears his girlfriend answer the question this way, and he has high integrity and is a basically honest person, he will be delighted. On the other hand, if the same guy hears his girlfriend respond in the manner of answerers two and three, he may lose some respect for her.

If she answered as did answerer number two, he may say to himself, "Hmm. The only reason she wouldn't cheat would be that she was afraid she wouldn't get the right answers that way. She's not really honest."

If she answered as did three, he would not only lose respect for her, he may seriously doubt their compatibility with one another. "She's a real skeptic, and an opportunist too. She would follow the crowd—everyone else does it, so that makes it all right." And he may find himself pulling away from her emotionally.

If he does pull away, what will have happened here is not sudden rejection decided in a fit of anger, but the realization that the two of them do not share certain values that are, to him, essential to a deepening relationship.

What? Am I telling you that if you don't watch out, you may lose your boyfriend or girlfriend? If this is so, should you be very cautious as you play the game, taking time to camouflage your answers so as not to let anyone know how you really feel? Of course not. That would defeat the very purpose of the game. You should instead dare to be yourself. After all, if your boyfriend or girlfriend can't cope with who you really are, aren't you much better off without him or her? And if you decide that you don't agree with your boyfriend or girlfriend on major issues, isn't it a lot better to find that out now rather than later, when you are married and may even have children together?

You know, the sad truth is, many couples do get married without having a clue as to how each other feels about moral issues. When these issues come up later in life—as they always do—wife and husband find themselves fighting to the point where divorce is inevitable. Before you marry, it would be a good preparation to play this game with your future spouse and find out where you stand.

Question from Chapter Four: Friends

8. If your friend were in a beauty or bodybuilding contest and you were one of the judges, and it came down to your vote deciding the contest, but your friend looked worse than the other contestants, would you vote for your friend or against her (him), knowing that your friend would never find out that it was your vote that decided the contest? Explain your answer.

Answer 1. "I'd vote for him. I'm loyal. And I'd expect him to do the same for me. Friends have to stick together."

Answer 2. "If I was sure she'd never find out, I'd vote for the best girl, but if I had any doubt that she might find out, I wouldn't have the heart to vote against her, because she wouldn't understand, and she'd think I betrayed her."

Answer 3. "I would vote against her. She shouldn't have been stupid enough to go into the contest looking bad, and anyway, what about the girl who deserved to win, and instead lost because I voted dishonestly? How would you or I like it if that happened to us? Friendship doesn't mean you have to abandon fairness and what's right and wrong. I'd be glad that she didn't know how I voted, but if she found out, I'd just tell her the truth."

If you would unquestioningly do anything for a friend, you would hope to have your bosom buddy answer in the manner of answerer number one. If, rather, your friend answers in the manner of answerer number two, you may think she's underhanded and two-faced. You may think, "How can I trust her? She doesn't really care about me, only that I don't find out that she betrayed me." On the other hand, you might understand her position, and appreciate her honesty in admitting what she would do.

If your friend answers in the manner of answerer number three, you may become angry and say to yourself, "Why does she have to be so self-righteous. Suddenly we have to worry about the justice in the world. I think it's only right to bend the rules when it comes to best friends." On the other hand, you learn from your friend's integrity, and wonder why you never realized that it is downright dishonest to vote for someone just because she is a friend.

In the end, you may alter you own opinion; but the point is, whether or not you eventually agree or disagree with your friend's answer to a question, that answer is food for thought. Rather than make snap judgments, think about what has been said. Allow your mind to digest the answers fully.

Question from Chapter Five: Teens Ask Parents

36. When you were a teen, did you ever feel ugly or inferior in any way? Explain your answer.

Answer 1. "I was always ten pounds overweight and they used to call me butterball. I didn't have as many dates as the other girls. Until I met your father, I never really felt pretty."

Answer 2. "I hated my nose. Even though my mother said it looked fine, I always thought it was too long, and it made me self-conscious with the girls. Later I seemed to forget about it—but I remember, now that you mention it, I never really felt handsome in my early high school years."

Answer 3. "Not really. I thought I looked pretty good, and if anyone didn't like me I didn't even notice it. It's not what's on the outside that counts anyway, but what's on the inside."

If your parent answers in the manner of answerer number one or number two, you'll probably see your parent in a different light. In fact, you may be surprised to realize that your parent in fact evolved into "parent" from very vulnerable teen.

This revelation may help you to realize that it's quite normal to have serious reservations about the acceptability of your looks during your teen years. In fact, when you think about it, you'll realize that if even your parents felt that way, and they eventually became adults, got married, and had children (as wonderful as you, in fact), you too probably will grow up into a normal, happy adult.

In addition, this revelation may help you to remember that your parent is not beyond feelings—and that he or she is something (maybe many things) besides an authority figure.

If your parent answers in the manner of number three, claiming never to have experienced feelings of insecurity regarding his or her looks, your parent is probably forgetting. That's easy enough to do. A person who has gone through a delicate stage in life and yet has become wise enough and secure enough to set priorities in order tends to forget the struggle it took to get there.

Parent number three can *now* confidently say, "It's what's inside that counts"—but rest assured, that conclusion was not reached without some painful teen experiences, and possibly some heart-to-heart talks with parents on the subject.

Another possibility is that your parent does clearly remember feelings of inferiority, but because those memories are too painful, he or she has buried them and they have become unconscious.

Other parents might deny having experienced insecurity over their looks because they fear that by admitting to a weakness, even though it was way back in their teen years, they may lose respect in their own teen's eyes. They opt to cover up their former feelings of inferiority in the hope of presenting what they intend to be a reassuringly strong front.

If your parent falls into this category, you may want to challenge him or her; but in any case, try to understand. That's the goal of the game anyway—not to change people, but to understand them and to have them understand us so that our relationships with them can improve.

Question from Chapter Six:
Parents Ask Teens

If I were to follow my usual procedure, I would give sample answers to a question in chapter six, then offer advice on interpreting the answers. Here, I can't do that.

The reason is clear. Although this section would be addressed to parents, you teens would read it (if for no other reason, out of curiosity). The end result would be to defeat the purpose of the game—to give open, honest answers. You would worry that your parent might interpret and analyze your answer a certain way. So I forgo a section advising parents on how to interpret various answers.

And to tell you the truth, parents don't really need my advice on how to interpret answers. The "school of life" has taught them enough so that they can do their own interpreting. However I do have a note for them, and if you wish, you may point it out to them before you begin the game.

A NOTE TO THE PARENTS

If you play the question game with your son or daughter, the key is to be calm and to resist the temptation, however strong, to attack your teen's answer. For example, do control yourself if your teen is presented with the question:

> "If you had an early curfew but wanted to go to a club far away, and you knew you wouldn't be home before 3:00, would you ask your parents if you could stay out later? Or would you ask permission to stay over at the house of someone you know has a later curfew?"

and your teen's answer is similar to this one:

"I would sleep over at someone's house so you would never really know what time I came home."

Rather than yield to your initial impulse to tell your son or daughter about your own detective work, store the information. Let your teen speak. Your reward will be continued open communication. By breaking in with warnings, sermons, and condemnations, you will force your teen to "clam up" for survival's sake.

Teens really do want to talk to parents, but so often, unwittingly, we force them into secrecy because of our reactions. It's not easy. I'm a parent of a teen also, and I often have to bite my tongue, but it's worth it. You can always have a heart-to-heart talk about issues of concern at an appropriate time.

Question from Chapter Seven:
Teens Ask Grandparents

35. Do you have any friends now? How many? Who is your best friend? Why is that person your best friend?

Answer 1. "I have about five close friends and about fifteen 'acquaintances,' who you could say are also friends. I don't really have a best friend. All of my close friends are best friends. I suppose I'm my own best friend."

Answer 2. "To be honest, I don't have any really good friends, just relatives that I'm close to and a few people I keep in touch with that I used to work with. I don't need a best friend at this age. I'm perfectly happy with life the way it is."

Answer 3. "When you get older, it's hard to keep your friends. Most of mine have moved far away, and many of them have died. I feel lonely and miss my friends—but there's nothing you can do about it. That's what happens when you get older."

If your grandparent answers in the manner of answerer number one, you may be surprised to learn that he or she has a going social life. You will be encouraged to know that when you get older, life does not stop. You'll also note that it is possible, with time and wisdom, to get to the place where you can be comfortable enough with yourself to say "I'm my own best friend." That's indeed something to look forward to.

If your grandparent is fortunate enough to feel the way number one does, you'll probably have positive thoughts about the time when you will be a grandparent. But more important, you will have learned something encouraging about your grandparent—that he or she is not only not to be pitied, but is to be, quite affirmatively, admired.

Grandparent number two reveals the difference of personalities in, yes, even grandparents. Just as younger people vary in their thinking and feelings, so too do older people. Some people tend to be content with family friendships as they get older, and to enjoy the closeness of the inner circle. They do not wish to venture out and make new friends, having lost, through attrition, the friends they had enjoyed in their youth.

If your grandparent answers in the manner of grandparent number two, you will learn that he or she is accepting of life, and rather happy and content with his or her lot. No need to feel sorry for this grandparent. Perhaps you will wonder how you will feel when you get older—whether you will join clubs and community groups, and expand your circle of friends, or whether you too will be content with your family and your own company. You may want to ask your grandparent why he or she does not join this or that travel club or senior citizen group. The answer will also give you insight.

Remember, the goal is not to change your grandparent (or anyone else for that matter) but rather to understand and build bridges of communication and acceptance.

If your grandparent answers as did grandparent number three, sadly, you will discover (perhaps to your surprise), that your grandparent is lonely. Although not a happy revelation, it can be an important one, especially if you decide to do something about it. You may determine to spend a little more time with your grandparent, and to find ways to include him or her in your life. You might also want to talk to your parents about what you have learned, and to discuss with them ways to help your grandparent to enjoy life to the fullest well into the autumn years.

Question from Chapter Eight:
Grandparents Ask Teens

Once again, I will not follow my usual procedure. If I give sample answers of teens answering grandparents, and then analyze these answers, you will probably read the answers even if I tell you not to—in fact, probably because I tell you not to. Any normal teenager would—out of sheer curiosity. But then you would not be able to play the game with spontaneity. You would be hampered by imagining how your grandparents are interpreting your answers.

Anyway, grandparents don't need any instructions on how to interpret your answers. In fact, I'm sure they could teach us both a thing or two. They're still trying to teach your parents, are they not?

Questions from Chapter Nine:
Ask Anyone About Anything

29. How many hours a week do you spend watching television? List three things you wish you had time to do. What would happen if you gave your television time to those things? How would you feel about yourself and your life? Why?

Answer 1. (adult co-worker) "I watch TV about four hours a day, or twenty-eight hours a week. I wish I had more time to work out in the gym, to study for a civil service exam, and to read. I would feel great if I could stop watching so much TV and start getting things done. I would be proud of myself, but I'm too lazy, so I just keep watching TV."

Answer 2. (parent of a friend) "I watch TV about fifteen hours a week, altogether. I work long hours, and when I come home I have to make dinner and clean up. Then I would like to read, or get things done, but I'm too tired. So I just sit on the couch and fall asleep watching TV. I put a lot of things off for the weekend, after I've got some rest. I'd feel great if I had the self-discipline to break my pattern."

Answer 3. (teacher) "I watch TV about eight hours a week. It's tempting just to sit in front of the tube for hours, but I have writing to do and papers to mark. When I'm finished with that, it comes down to watching TV, reading a good book, or doing work for a course I'm taking. I've accomplished so much with time I used to waste watching TV, that I'm really careful not to fall back into that trap."

All three answers provide information on how different people deal with the problem of the lure of television. The end result can be a learning experience.

The co-worker reminds one of how television can steal valued time that could be better spent achieving goals. I'm sure that some of the players listening to number one might say, "I do that, too. I'd better stop letting my life slip away as I sit in front of that tube."

The parent of a friend points out a truth about television: It's a vehicle for sheer vegetation when we are exhausted. What could be more convenient than plopping down on the couch, where neither thinking nor moving is required? The only trouble is, if we do that every time we are tired, we will have to do a lot of neglected chores on the week-end. Some players might think, "I'll make it my business to resist that temptation, no matter how tired I am." Others might gain comfort in knowing they are not alone, and continue to do just what they're doing.

The teacher sets the best example, showing that television viewing can be held in check. Some players might attribute the self-discipline of number three to the fact that she is a teacher. "Teachers have more self-control," they might say. "If I try it, it just won't work." On the other hand, some players may become inspired by the teacher's example, and say to themselves, "If even teachers are tempted, I don't feel so bad. Maybe I too can resist the pull of the television."

The point is, by listening to other players' answers, we can compare and contrast what they say to our own situation. We can gain comfort, learn from their mistakes, or, quietly or blatantly, disagree. The important thing is, we are thinking.

We are growing mentally.

ARE YOU OPINIONATED?

As mentioned in chapter one, to be opinionated is to hold unreasonably or obstinately to your own idea—and not only to refuse to consider another point of view, but to refuse to allow another point of view to exist, to the point where you judge or condemn the person for even having a different opinion—specifically, one that is offensive to you.

One of the goals of the question game is to help you to be less opinionated. If you find yourself condemning others because they don't agree with you, chances are you are at least somewhat "opinionated."

Any player who attacks another with phrases such as, "You idiot. How can you be so stupid?" or, "That's ridiculous," or any phrases that suggest complete intolerance of opposing opinions, must—as mentioned in question-game rule four, page 12, —read the following passage out loud:

> I have rules about the way people must think. If they do not follow my rules, they are stupid. Wait a minute. What am I saying? This is ridiculous. Everyone has a right to his or her opinion. I have a right to mine. It may be unpleasant to hear a viewpoint that is different or even opposite from my own, but I now realize that there's no reason to feel threatened if such opinions are voiced. In fact, I can learn to enjoy hearing opposing points of view because I can gain insight into other people's thinking. In the end, I am not forced to change my opinion, but who knows, I may. In any case, there is no danger to me in hearing what other people have to say.

What's the point of having players read the above passage? In reading the passage, the player will see how irrational it is to behave in a manner that assumes omniscience (exclusive knowledge of all truth). He or she will realize that there is no danger in allowing other points of view to be expressed, and will realize that it is not his or her job to keep the world safe from opinions that do not coincide with his or hers. This player will eventually become more relaxed, and will probably eventually enjoy a wider circle of friends.

AN INVITATION

I hope you've enjoyed playing the question game. I'd like to know what has happened to you as a result of playing the game. If you have anything to tell me regarding new friends you've made, revelations you've got that have caused you to take action, or any other special insights or experiences, please write to me. If you wish a response, please include a stamped, self-addressed envelope.

Also, if you have a good question that was not asked in this book and you wish to share it with others, please send it to me.

> JOYCE L. VEDRAL
> P.O. Box A 433
> Wantagh, NY 11793-0433

– ABOUT THE AUTHOR'S OTHER WORKS –

Books for Teens

My Teacher Is Driving Me Crazy Attention: high school and junior high school students who want to find out how to pass the course and get the best grade possible, no matter what the teacher is like. This book deals with teachers of every kind, including boring, unfair, burned out, out of control, and rigid; talks about wonderful teachers and shows why dedicated teachers remain, despite the difficulties; gives you insight into why teachers behave the way they do and instruction on how to get fair treatment from them. Joyce Vedral, teaching veteran of twenty-five years, gives away secrets. Learn what goes on behind the scenes; learn how your teachers are treated by *their* superiors!

Boyfriends: Getting Them, Keeping Them, Living without Them shows the teenage girl how to attract and keep the attention of the guy she has in mind; suggests ways to "make the first move" without seeming obvious; looks into the insecurities of guys and shows girls what is really behind some of their angry words and deeds; talks about how sex changes the relationship, and about why guys sometimes break up with girls shortly after sex enters the picture; gives advice on what to do in such a situation; helps girls not only to get over a broken heart, but to find ways to enjoy life even more after the breakup; helps to build self-confidence and self-esteem.

The Opposite Sex Is Driving Me Crazy helps you understand why the opposite sex behaves the way it does. The book is divided into halves: Girls answer favorite questions posed by boys; boys answer typical questions asked by girls. Covered are such topics as jealousy and cheating, sex, spending time and money, turn-ons and turn-offs, and favorite lectures mothers and fathers give sons and daughters. Teens are helped to realize that they are not "weird," that they are not "rejects"—and they are given ways to deal with even the most cruel behavior of the opposite sex. The tone is humor with generous sprinklings of love, wisdom, and common sense.

My Parents Are Driving Me Crazy gives you, the teenager, insight into the workings of the adult—specifically parent—mind; it helps you to become more loving, compassionate, and understanding of your parents. Teens who have read the book often report that it has totally changed their relationship with their parents.

My Teenager Is Driving Me Crazy is a book for your parents if you want them to understand what goes through your mind when you do certain outrageous things—things like coming home late, telling them how to dress and behave, borrowing their things without asking, hanging out with the "wrong crowd," neglecting important chores, etc. This short course on the teenage mind tells parents what you really worry about; helps them learn how to listen to you without interrupting with a lecture, and how to talk to you so you'll listen; let's them know that all their hard work is not in vain, and that many of their values really are getting through to you, even though they may not see the clear and convincing evidence of that until you're an adult. The book gives specific examples of when a teen was about to do "the wrong thing," but stopped himself because his parents' words came to mind.

I Can't Take It Any More In its deepest intent a suicide prevention guide, this book aims to help all teens learn how to deal with anger, rage, hate, fear, anguish of rejection, and other negative emotions that otherwise could blight, if not destroy, lives. This guide shows you how to channel such powerful emotions toward affirmative goals you can achieve instead of turning them inward against the self. Many young adults have written that the words from this book have come back to them and helped them to go on when they were feeling down or even having suicidal thoughts.

I Dare You Here is a *How to Win Friends and Influence People* for teenagers. It motivates you to overcome obstacles and achieve goals, and shows you how to use psychology in dealing with teachers, bosses, and other authorities and friends in order to help make things run more smoothly.

Fitness Books

The Fat-Burning Workout is a twenty-minute weight training program that reshapes the body and burns body fat; a low-fat eating plan is also provided. It is excellent for teens as well as adults, who want to stay in shape and eat well at the same time. (Warner Books, 1991)

The Twelve-Minute Total-Body Workout An intense exercise program for busy teenagers and adults, this workout requires only twelve minutes a day and a pair of three-pound dumbbells. It includes a nutritious diet that helps exercisers lose excess body fat without sacrificing good nutrition. (Warner Books, 1989)

Any of the teen books can be ordered by calling the toll-free number at Ballantine Books: 1-800-733-3000. The fitness books can by purchased in major bookstores.

Joyce Vedral is also author or coauthor of several other fitness and diet books:

Bottoms Up
Now or Never
Cameo Fitness with Cameo Kneuer
Perfect Parts with Rachel McLish

Hard Bodies with Gladys Portugues
The Hard Bodies Express Workout with Gladys Portugues
Supercut: Nutrition for the Ultimate Physique
Gut Busters

Also by

JOYCE VEDRAL

Available at bookstores everywhere.
Published by Ballantine Books.